The Circle of
SEASONS

The Circle of

SEASONS

Photographs by Dennis Stock
Text by Josephine W. Johnson

A STUDIO BOOK · THE VIKING PRESS · NEW YORK

To my mother

D. S.

CONTENTS

THE SEASONS

Winds circle the world. The seasons flow, bearing their tides of seed, blue waters, darkening mists, the cry of gulls. Gold hails of light will follow rain. The seasons are a vast living wreath of light and scent and sound, so densely woven there is no end and no beginning. The hummingbird flies two thousand miles, a small burning thread of light, following the silver needle of its beak to drink spring honey from cold early flowers. And then returns two thousand miles when the season of flowers is over.

SPRING

Along water courses in the early hours of spring rise curious pale shell-colored things, blind big-headed plants on transparent stems. It comes alone, this parent plant of the common horse-tail, the equisetum, fragile and potent, pushing its way through blue clay and sand. Its stem is notched and jointed, section set into section, and around the solitary parent plant rushes up a forest of bristly green and beautiful little trees—the sterile shoots from the same underground stem. This small forest, the equisetum, is as old as the world, and circles the world. In the Asian springs, and the springs of Europe, these strange pale heads arise, and the green bristles follow. Once they were true forests, enormous fern trees, the jungles of Carboniferous time, and older than the first little horse which trotted on four toes. Now they are pine trees only to the black spring frogs, enormous only to the small brown burning shrews.

In the early spring the trees are gray and cold. The grayness seems to last forever. Gray etchings such as one sees in old books, grim primer readers. Bare structure of a loom. Then the birds begin to weave the first bright fiery threads. Up from Bolivia, Peru, from Cuba and Mexico and Colombia—arrows and needles of light. The tanager blazes against the blue sky. A red glow like a star in the bare branches, rose and orange-red. A startling color for early spring. And tanagers with black wings, a lump of coal bursting into flame. The bluebirds come. Sit thoughtfully with large dome-shaped heads, balancing themselves on the barren twigs. Blue as the shadows of late winter snow.

In the bare trees of early spring one can still see old oak galls lumpy against the sky, and the nests of blue gnatcatchers, silvery lumps like the galls, are built early and with incessant sound, high and shrill in the chilly winds. *Chebec, chebec, chip-chip-chip*—almost a whine. Smallest king-of-the-mosquitoes, Empidonax minimus, up from Mexico to build its webbed and silver-lichened nest. A little bird gray as the branches in shadow, blue in the sunlight.

In the far north, in Alaska, birds cover the cliffs in place of leaves. Wings cover the rocks. Bird flocks are fields of flowers in the early hours of spring. Green water, green moss, and then the greening of the northern springs.

The life of spring is an uncoiling. The bear, coiled like a great fur pill bug in winter, stretches and rises. The silver and brown heads of ferns—fiddleheads, crosiers—are emerging. Slowly the shape uncoils and uncoils, until the last frosty brown fist opens and greens. Like green caterpillars, the ferns stretch out into beautiful green wings. Pteridophyta, wings, the world of ferns, the world of wings that covers—once covered Asia, Europe, the new world, but not the world to come.

Out of the cold blue valleys the mists of morning rise as from the oceans long ago. Spring is cold and hoarse. Its rains are gentle, and then they pierce the marrow, immobilize the passive frogs, cool all things down and down, wash the rocks and sluice the naked clay. To those early beings who emerged from cold caves to cold skies, there was only the first blue crayfish to be found. Hungry and scrawny, they scrounged the rocks, turning them over as the raccoons turn them now, eating green buds, raw roots, good or bad, poison or life-giving, by trial and error. It took a little shorter to die of wrong choices then.

Slowly in the cold are beautiful and small beginnings. In shallow streams the little dagger of salamander efts, fringed embryos. In moss and black earth the scarlet cups of fungus under leaves. Water runs over the silent rocks, the lichen lives again and greens, and thus rocks feel the spring. Feel the feet of emerald hunting beetles, and are marked by wandering silver script of snails. Amoeba spring. The good green germs! Through a thousand springs who rules what rises from the dark cool roots of things? The sound of small streams in the small ravines, the cool sound of water pouring over stones, seeking its own level. The water sound of leaves—the soothing soft swish of the leaves.

The light of early spring is a filtered light, a mesh light, that comes through the first fine net of leaves covering the old gray nerves of twigs. A net of small wet leaves, gold and red before their greening. And the shadow of these earliest of leaves, the buckeye chestnut, whose leaf clusters look like red—dark red—chrysanthemum flowers—these shadows are sharp and delicate against the silver trunk of a bark-stripped tree. When all the other trees are bare, these shadows are cast against the tree, and move in wind, sharp and distinct as bird feet on the silver aging wood.

Lovely, this light of spring shining through delicate green leaves, small silver leaves of oak and sycamore, copper foil of the beech unfolding, shining through the dust of pollen, the windy flight of pollen, the gold haze of arboreal spring.

An indefinable and lovely scent comes in the air. Almost invisible flowers among the forest leaves are sweet as plums. In the desert, along the dry arroyos, one lonely bush gives off that same wandering honey scent—the essence of returning spring before the waves of desert flowers. Rain falls in the dry sweet desert air. Cool scent of dust and sage between enormous drops. The dry lands, the clay and sand, boil up flowers. Mists and lakes of blue lupin flow between earth and sky. The fields of wild poppy are a sunset fire.

How can I go on telling about all this, and underneath, the voice crying, "It is going, it is going." . . . It was, but it is no more, never again. The great garland is fraying, is dying, torn apart. The tapestry knifed. The vandals prosper . . . death around the world.

The hummingbird comes through the cold untimely rain. His flight a burning thread. Two thousand miles this little thing has come. It is not *ours*—it is not *theirs*—it is its own. But the world is round; the world is woven like a web. The blind reach out with giant knives and cut this beautiful and blazing thread. Atropos, the old Fate with the shears. The world is full of blind old beings with big shears—the Atropoi. Engineers, officers, scientists, and politicians—they study the seasons, but not as the farmer studies the seasons for life. They study the seasonal floods so they can impound them, the seasonal rains so they can bomb between them, the habits of birds so that they may spy with them, the habits of dolphins so they may arm them and kill with them, and they study the clouds to use them for destruction. All knowledge, all that lives or exists is examined in the light of its use as an instrument of destruction—and the moon is their landscape, their ideal, and their nature. It is white and neat and dead.

The tides of spring wash north. A necklace of frogs forms around the ponds. The spruce trees are full of sweetness, full of bees and flies. The great trees hum and sizzle with insects. Sough with wind like a green heavy surf. The new green of their spring needles is soft and rubbery, spry as little plumes and feathers. One small tree is covered over like a bird.

A single lonely-looking pear blooms in the steep woods. Planted by a bird, it is long and striving up thin like the other trees of the forest. Pared narrow by reaching for light. It has white fragrant blossoms and incomparable bronze-green leaves. There is nothing more beautiful than a spring pear leaf. The blossoms of this pear tree are unreachable—a high and solitary bouquet in the gray woods. So high I thought no pears ever developed from these flowers. It seemed to have gone wild and self-sustaining, having no future but its own. But one summer, out of the rain and filtered sunlight, it created, squeezed into life, five infinitesimal green pears. Swallows can harvest this fruit up near the stars.

In the green pastures life flows through the horses. The heavy life ripple of their muscles, the moist soft twitching of their noses. There is a delicate unbalance in the early foals; a soft snorting sound comes from their grazing muzzles. And there is a flowing balance in the marvelous arch of a horse's neck—that shining arch of strength and curve almost beyond comparison with any other living thing.

The smell of horses is rich, a strong animal fragrance, but the softness of their noses reminds one of flowers, of the soft suede pinkness of magnolia blossoms, that large and luscious flower of early spring with its great pink petals, its opening and falling shell-pink petals. In the cold springs of the Midwest these flowers seemed tropical, exotic, their cream-and-rose petals almost sinister. Not domesticated as the rose—not understandable as the rose is understood. Their elusive scent was offbeat, not easily defined. But it brings back childhood and the heartbreaking sound of robins singing in the gray warm evenings. One gathered the browning petals from the grass, one never picked a blossom off the tree. Tree and blossom were all one—and trees were not made for the making of bouquets.

Magnolias open all over the temperate and tropical worlds, and once they were flowers of Siberia and Greenland—long-vanished wild gardens deep under the snow, the petals turned to stone. The sweet-bay magnolia is fragrant in the southern swamps, and the spoonbill stork's great rose-colored body blooms like a living saucer magnolia, beautiful and odd on its long stem legs above the blue water.

More than two thousand years ago when Hesiod wrote about the seasons, he marked the coming of spring by the migration of the cranes, and the rare whooping cranes of Texas, the great tall birds with long windpipes coiled in the hollow of their breastbones, fly north in their own mysterious migration to nest somewhere in the Arctic. In the middle states the little blue and green herons, rusty-breasted, invisible among the willows, croak above the ponds and cattails. Scrunched up and hoarse, the heron waits and watches. At last a huge frog voice rumbles up from the water. Its voice is huge and pretentious. "What're we to do? What're we to do?" it bellows in grave anguish.

14

Strange days come in early spring. Snow storms sweep the northern plains. Frost lies on Florida. In the sheltered Midwest violent changes twist the slow-rising April. Rain, wind, and lightning, then a freezing chill. The stiff vines swing like wires, each with an ice bulb on the end. On the blue beach delicate ice drops freeze. Ice ferns, ice slush on the windows. The ground looks white and barren, as though the white sands of Virginia Beach had blown far inland. Goldfinches and rose finches huddle in the bush that has flowers of ice instead of flowers of honey. The cardinal's Day-Glo red flames out above the piles of slushy hail. The frozen branches scratch the pane, make icy snarls as from opossums' rattling teeth. And the daffodils droop green and gold above the white untimely ice.

And then the sun returns, the ice is April water, and the grass rushes up on a tide of its own. The balance tips, vibrates, evens out, is never still. Marvelous are the deceptions and disguises of the natural world. The guises and changes that hold the balance. A spring rampant with aphids brings its lady beetles—brings also some that seem lady beetles of enormous and unnatural size. The eggs are laid as lady beetles lay their eggs, neat capsules, shining orange, placed in rows. And then things humped and horrendous emerge from the neat pill eggs. The orange capsules walk off on legs, they wear black masks, they look like grubs with red turtle shells. They are some species of leaf-eating beetle, enormous vegetarians. They are not lady beetles at all.

The great moths emerge. The luna comes with breathtaking loveliness, a green and delicate moth out of a white and silver cocoon, spun by a green and pig-size caterpillar. A vast rearrangement of matter to bring this green and silver, this white furred moth, out of its last year's eating chunk. Up from the pine-needled earth, out of its dark strict cell, its winter of silence, the Empress moth struggles into the light, unfolds and dries its pale yellow wings—wings watermarked with lavender. Then lies huge and exhausted by birth, resting on the cool stones in the morning light. Small owlet butterflies flicker in spring woods, but the earliest butterfly is the mourning-cloak, a thing of such remarkable beauty, of such subtle wine-red color running down to heavy cream, that an unreasonable jealousy rises in one—both jealousy and awe, for this frail velvet thing lives through the winter, hibernates, and comes alive in the first warm day of spring.

Butterflies and moths grow scarcer, rarer, and more rare. In my childhood they were a part of life—part of the whole that was spring and summer in the world. Not just in the country, but in all small towns. Butterflies and flowers, and birds and stars. Horses in the pastures. Now the huge highway lights go up, the supermarket lights burn late. The lights blot out the stars.

The moths burn up. Will our children see the stars? Our children's children? Not for them. Will our children know real quietness? That background for small sounds—the small sound of a bee, the summer buzzing of a fly? The highway sounds devour all little sounds. Will there be any rhythm and difference of season left, any feeling of the great circular flow of living things?

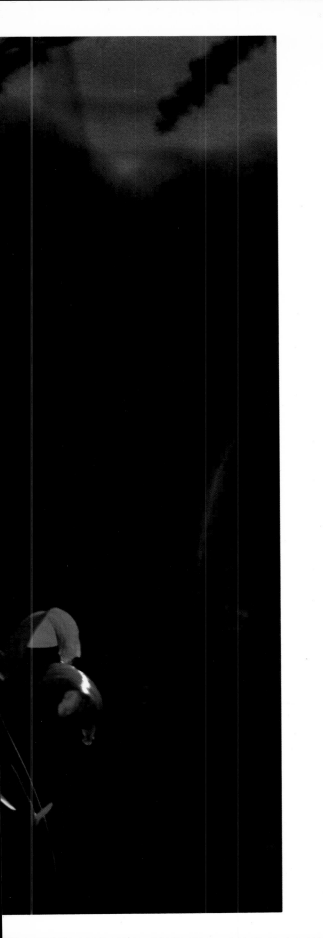

SUMMER

At some hour there comes a change, a difference in the air, a difference in the light. It is a strange and indefinable turning, a presence arriving, as a deer is there in a clearing where there was no deer before. It is the drying of the air, the broken blades of grass, and the scent of roses. Summer is the world of roses. White brier roses, small and sharply sweet, hedges and fountains of multiflora roses, and the satin-petaled garden roses that drip with dew. Gardens of roses and fountains were promised to the faithful in the heaven of the Koran. "Which one of your Lord's blessings will you ungratefully deny?" asks Mohammed. Not the warm and wonderful, the full sweet scent of roses that softens and spreads across the changing air. A scent different in every way from the cool, almost root-sweet scent of the spring magnolias; it is the difference between spring and summer air.

The endless weaving across the continent, across the world, goes on. Long silver threads of spiders in the sunlight. The spiraling sound of cicadas drilling through the heat. The cuckoo jeers, "*Talk-talk-talk. Talk-talk-talk.*" The fish weave patterns in the ponds, small wavings, muddy gold fins. The dragonflies crackle. A sound of burning paper. The light shines through their glassy veins. The swallows swoop and weave and rise, circle the world with their wings. The young swallows seem *chased* by their parents—fly or die, swoop or swim, follow the pattern of the gnats, the silver whining trails of mosquitoes. In the last darkening hours they finally rest on willow limbs or in old barn eaves. The frogs have certain spaced positions around the ponds. They sit in wet armor, a necklace, a ring of wet coal lumps. They ingest the dancing silver swarms of gnats and mosquitoes, the weary fly. The frogs are taught by their inner parents, the cold, resident instincts. Sit still—or die. Swoop—and you starve. Let the swallows chase your dinner down low. Wait and watch! Huge and beautiful, life-giving, are those gold-rimmed staring eyes.

The mulberry tree flashes like a yule tree with the light of wings. It is a magnet for all birds. Hooks them! Brings them back, hour after hour, until the last fruit is gone. Even the sourest late green berry. Yellow-breasted chats hang like gold pears. The red-bellied woodpeckers blunder in the lower branches; the cedar waxwings crest at the top against the sky. The mulberry twigs swing up and down under the chipmunks' feet, under the goldfinches, indigo buntings blue as jewels, under the redbirds, the cardinals which are everywhere, bright burning red. Suddenly the whole tree seems to explode, is torn apart by the great shining ebony wings of a crow. Then the leaves fall back in place, the purple fruit, rose-red, green-red, stops shaking. Slowly the birds return.

The white mulberry tree is second choice; the pale, wormlike pearls of fruit do not excite the eye. But it grows around the world. It came—or was brought—in sailing ships from China where great plantations were grown to feed the silkworm caterpillars. Strange to think of all those green leaves turning into threads, flowing out in long silky threads—a thousand feet of silk for every round one-inch cocoon, a thousand miles of silk for every pound. Bombyx mori, white moth and white cocoon. The mulberry tree spread out across the states, but the silkworm did not follow. It needed a quiet sheltered life—protection for its art.

Marmots—woodchucks and prairie dogs, ground squirrels and chipmunks—are out from coast to coast. The woodchuck shovels in long grass, new goldenrod, large violet leaves. The hair on his forehead is purple, his eyes are dark and cloudy. His fur grows in concentric circles and, in certain lights, he is looped with silver hair. Odd fur halos that come and go. He eats and listens, eats and listens. He chews six seconds, listens seven. He lives in a constant state of apprehension, but it is not like ours. His digestion is good. It serves him well. Mountains of violet leaves go down. The woodchuck is not a marmot for all seasons; his blood is bound by falling temperatures and falling light. A mellow tallow fills his mind, and by Thanksgiving he is blotted out. But now in summer he can still bound, make leaps like a football bouncing, and climb trees if so inclined.

The woodcock flies over the woodchuck's head; it has a veering, leaf-twirling flight and cry. And at night makes piercing, peeping sounds, spring cries like little knives.

The wrens carry leaves like banners in the nest-building rituals. Does this please you, my love? . . . or this? . . . or this? One bore a silver seed of lunaria in its beak. (Honesty it is called sometimes—moonwort, satinpod—but mostly "The Money Plant.") The sun shone through the pale transparent seed, two pennies left inside. It drifted down. It had not pleased her. Even in the high hot tide of summer there are silver hours. Early morning and the dew silvering every hair and prickle of the thistle leaves. (Summer, Hesiod said, is marked by the blooming of the thistle, but the farmer hopes to know his summer by almost any other sign.) The pale treehoppers perch in frosted rows. The grapevines have white-silver leaves. The pasture cedars huddle in herds, silver-haired and shaggy as the Old Man cactus, when the night dew is heavy, cooling down the hot scent, sexy and pervasive, the cedar scent delicate as a musky net. The spider webs are everywhere, transparent silver disks among the sea of wild carrot blooms. A snail trail wanders over a web. Did it bounce like a trampoline under this wandering, gluey weight? . . . These webs in the grass, in the trees, in the twigs and pathways, these delicate silver-thread weavings for death and for food—flat in the face you get them; white threads drip around your ears.

The sun is higher—or earth is farther—the air changes. Puffs of damp air come out from under the leaves, and then the night odors leave. The blue haze across the valley changes to dust blue. Even the dew seems warmer. Darning needles pierce the drops, and, in each drop of dew, there seems to be a smiling chigger's face.

The dock—big burdock, jungle size—has a vibrant thrust and power. The stems are vigorous, the pathways of its veining strong. But the inner leaves are green and silver, soft and velvet as a toad's stomach, beautifully curled and secret. Cut the burdock back and it grows a thousand compensations. Seed-bearing horns, purple flowers, gross prickly packages of life that cling with teeth and hook and claw—a vegetable passion.

The locust leaves fall early. A delicate wandering rain of gold. The honey locust is a brittle tree, brittle branches, shedding leaves, shedding blossoms of marvelous fragrance—white and gold. But its body is a mass of thorns, small vicious warty thorns, great visible clumps of thorns, mean, hidden thorns along its bark. Once a whole locust seemed to die. Shed its leaves, lost its bark, turned dry silver, was burrowed in, full of holes, inhabited by starlings. And then one spring, out of this utterly leafless, barkless tree, far up near the sky, sprouted out from the trunk itself long fragrant white blossoms, astonishing as an old man's child! (But that was it. Then it really died.)

We think of our own four periods of climate as somehow the way things are and should be always, but much of the world has two seasons only, the wet season and the dry. Wet seasons strike us out of time. Late, cold. The old dry days of summer seem gone in some of the heartland states. Cold rain pours over the cold green leaves, over the tropical rampant growth of vines, whose virile green used to shrivel and brown in the old days. The cold rain chills the green to blue, sends the algae cowering out of sight in the ponds. Strange storms come. At three in the afternoon the north sky is red and then turns dusty yellow. The sky grows dark as evening. The winds howl like wolves. The trees labor in the wind, and the wind scythes up and down the valley. A locust tree cracks and shoots up splinters sharp as orange knives. The thunder is continuous for an hour. Impersonal and majestic. Glass bullets of hail pour down. And then, after the storm birth and excitement, the rain comes—a cold and miserable afterbirth sliding down. At the end, when it is all over, a strange evil bird arrives—a Bosch bird. Something born of a polluted egg somewhere.

All of the seasons have ragged edges. They are full of beginnings, half-finished things, untimely endings. The young of the cardinals come in half red, splotchy yellow, porcupine feathers, short tails, big bills. Their flying is a splatter. Young robins are feathered wildly. There is so much going on on a young robin. White dots, parentheses, exclamation points, dashes of white and black around their great eyes. White and lavender spots over the brown clay-colored feathers. And then something goes running through these threadlike plumes; the brown clay color turns to terra cotta, the feathers darken into black, and all the mysterious squiggles, all the unfinished messages, are blotted out. The known and calm, the adult robin, has arrived.

Left alone and not too sorely wounded, the natural world restores itself, corrects its own internal wars. One winter deep and untimely cold made a great honeysuckle kill. Acres of honeysuckle, green still in December—honeysuckle whose plan to take over the Midwestern world was going well—was overnight turned to frosted mush. The leaves fell off and a smell of silos followed, the strange odor of green dying. Then it all browned, and where the waves of green had been were mats of brown seaweed, herds of brown buffalo—one of the vastest, most selective kills of all the year. But all things move, restore. The vast weaving fills, and under the mats of honeysuckle an ancient Concord grapevine, which had struggled for fifty years to live unaided, crept out. Its small rose and silver leaves pushed out of the wiry web of dead vines, grew huge and green, and produced a hundred bunches of grapes, green in August, turning purple—an extraordinary harvest resurgence after its years of suppressed and shadowed life.

The skies of summer hold great oceans. Waves and crests of waves hold great dreaming drifts of warm snow, heads of white buffalo. Children should know the clouds, read the skies. Classes should be let out on great cloud days in all seasons. The coming of a storm is an event, a great drama. Under the huge skies of the West one can stand and see storms miles away, cloud pageants rolling. Fiery seas that seem to boil up from the fiery heart of the earth itself. This great piling and dissolving, these thousand shapes, have form and pattern and meaning—but never the same twice over.

Nobody can leave a cloud alone to be a cloud. . . . It is the size of a man's hand, the Bible says. . . . It is a white chicken, a rabbit's tail, a pinch of heroin, a splatter of cotton. *Cirrus* —to curl . . . cat's tail . . . mare's tail. *Cirrocumulus* makes a mackerel sky—shoals of white fish portending rain. . . . *Cumulus humilis* rising slowly to *cumulonimbus* bringing storms. And the strange clouds of *Cumulonimbus mamma*, seldom seen, great gray sagging cobwebs, portending tornadoes, thunderstorms. Sky-covering clouds, ominous and low, that stretched across the farms in Missouri, frightening as being trapped under a falling tent or a falling elephant.

Summer and warmth and clouds. White clouds that move and dissolve, take the shape of continents, move as the great land continents once moved. Africa and America once joined together . . . drifted apart. The light of summer is a forever-changing light. It shines and glitters on wasp wings, makes the water shine and glitter as scales of fish. And sometimes, on summer afternoons, there is a rare, desert-tent light, a curious yellow light as though great tented veils hung between earth and the sun. An unearthly light as in a yellow dream—and no rain follows.

In the summer evenings fireflies light the soybean fields. Millions—as though a green log had broken open and the sparks flew out.

Sometimes in summer evenings fogs roll in. Even inland fogs make valleys steam and boil. The mists come in the windows, fill the lungs. The tops of trees seem an island in the mist. So thick the fog one could row across the valley to the home on the other ridge. Never have I seen such thick whiteness! Dreamlike, I could see little Jamey and her mother in a canoe, paddling among the fog waves—then the waves rose, covered the trees, covered the whole valley, and carried the canoe home over the horizon in a storm of mist.

A beetle thing came flying past. I swear it flew upright, like a little man, its feet dangling toward the earth, its arms flailing madly, the sound like the sound of a miniature motorbike. The beetle was large and dark and seemed as though it knew its motor would run down, its spring unwind, and it would crash and everyone would laugh. It was a desperate flight. They say the ground beetle does not fly often, and this would, indeed, seem true.

The evening brings its evening sounds. Sounds like a crocodile arriving over a rocky beach, as the raccoon family descends the scaly cherry tree. The sounds of katydids and crickets—the soft whirr of the evening moth—the runnyduke of frogs. Silence and the wind in the fir trees, and then a sudden loud ululation, howls, like a pack of dogs, someone shouting gibberish

35

through a loudspeaker, and the sound of two people trying to speak through bandaged mouths.
. . . It is only the owls. They have conversed and gone. The quiet comes again.

The quail come creeping. The young all feathered now, with small lavender tails. Little copies of the parent quail. Exact miniatures, with all the elaborate markings—that unbelievable layer of feather on feather on feather, brown shading into black, into white, into yellow, into dust purple. They gather bugs like grain.

The gentian is deep blue, blue as the hill shadows in the mountains of New England. The goldenrod begins its bright and sunny blooming. The nights chill down. The saw-whet owls complain—or speak together—in the dark, an insect sound. Anxiety is in the air, in the human heart. The balance of the year begins to slide—a change is coming. How in God's name can the hummingbird store up enough fat cells, gold bricks, to fly those thousands of miles again? What's happening inside, what gives the signal—no more jewelweed, no more lilies, pollen of ragweed dispersed on the wind? The rubythroat dips so deep in the bergamot it flies off with a purple flower on its beak, then drops it like an empty cup in the wind. Green nuts are falling. Green hickory, compact, soft green leather—green walnuts, hard, gravelly, aromatic as spice.

August, late August, and the summer fading in the morning fogs along the Atlantic coast. The last surf rider in the mist, the beach plums wet with mist. Winds driving inland, and the cold sea rains. Then sunlight and the sound of waves.

The waves roll up the beach, cover the gold and green and snail-encrusted rocks, pour back with a strange rushing sound of teeth on stone, leave pools of starfish feeling delicately about, jellyfish, hermit crabs. The sea supports the gold-eyed gulls, heaves its enormous silver skin between the sky and shore, shudders and foams, pours over the moonstone rocks—neither knows nor cares that the summer people have all gone home. Along the back roads the great ferns turn gold, the pink mallows bloom and close.

Now summer ends as in years past. The nights grow colder, then warm nights return, then colder . . . like a tame thing going wild which stays away longer and longer, comes back briefly, plays and eats as before, but with abstraction in its eyes. Each return is briefer, cooler. . . . What am I doing here? . . . What did I ever see in this place? . . . Its teeth are sharper and its heart withdraws. And then, some night, it is not summer any more.

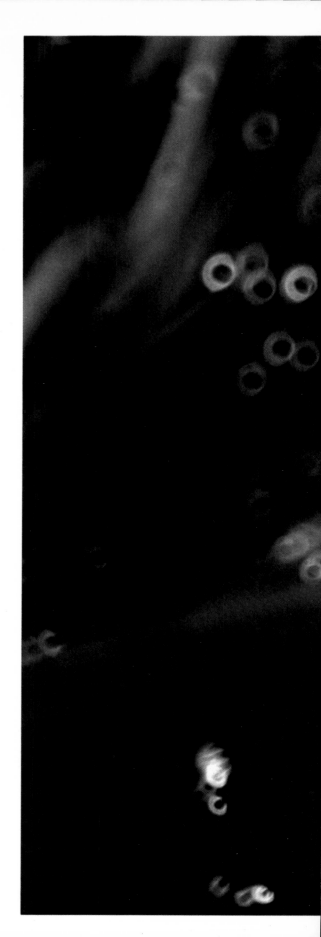

AUTUMN

Now is the hour of the earthly sun. The upsurge of yellow. Gold in all its forms and shades, the harvest of yellow flowers. A multitude of fallen suns along the creeks and ditches, railroad tracks and open plains. Sunflowers of every size and name, of the shape that children draw the sun. Tough hairy stems, stems bearing rough gold-yellow heads, the great, worldwide family of the Compositae—the all-together plants, the brilliant, tough, and well composed.

Red-gold gaillardias are small sunsets in the fields, Indian blankets, and along the streams and bottom lands the fringed suns of the elecampane grow with monstrous great green leaves. In the fields the domesticated giant sunflower spreads its simple-minded, heavy-headed orb, patiently turning as the earth turns, following its leash of light, its stout neck bending and bending as its face spreads out. One foot . . . two feet . . . stretching and stretching to become an earthly sun. And then the light-leash breaks. The real, the master sun, is too far away. Ambitions done. The disk flowers turn into a honeycomb of seeds, the big head falls upon its chin. Goldfinches come, cover the big brown platters. Feast.

Cherish the sunlight. The sun's not leaving us—our world is turning away from it. Whirling all us poor pushpins farther and farther from its great beneficence. An old man follows the sunlight around and around the house wall. Follows the red heart, the gold engine of all life. Under the sun the snow of mountain peaks is blinding bright, the sky beyond a blinding blue. Sun shines on the valleys of aspen turned to gold, sun shines on the fields of stubble, the great shorn coat of grain. Sun pours through the maple leaves with a red and rushing sound. The tulip trees are yellow. Shimmer like water in the wind. Tulip seeds whirl down a wedge-shaped formation like airplanes diving toward the earth, seemingly winged as birds, but on the ground—just a slip of a thing, no wings at all.

The morning glory blooms once more. One large frail glory blue as the sky among its fading yellow leaves. The great mantises disappear as their food dwindles, their house of eggs exuded, established in fields of goldenrod. The early green-yellow of the goldenrod now burns up into pure yellow plumes. The name for goldenrod is *Solidago*—to strengthen and unite—and the fields of plumes are brave-looking, strong-stemmed and woody, the fragrance is strong, wild and autumnal. There is not just one goldenrod, one classic plume-shaped flower. Goldenrod is wand-shaped in the woods, delicate as a spring flower there, with its trace of gold wandering up and down the stem. And there are late goldenrod and early, tall solidago, sweet solidago, rough-stemmed goldenrod . . . bog, pine-barren, rough-leaved, elm-leaved, zigzag, showy, flat-topped, slender, lance-leaved, and solidago gray.

Some are stout and some are noble—and then one day they are *all* gray. Beautiful old plumes of gray, surfing like winter seas in the north wind.

Autumn comes early in the mountains. Moves south and eastward. Slow and inexorable. Beautiful rivers of red-gold pour through the trees. The washed gold leaves more beautiful than any gold specks in a mountain stream. And now the gold trees go down and down. Concrete and asphalt swarm with metallic insect life of cars, each beating with a tiny man-heart in its padded cell.

The mountain covey makes its little pile of hay and gathers in its harvest. The mountain sheep come down. In crevices and little caves the lady beetles gather and ball up and sleep. The blazing leaves no longer breathe. No smoke rises from these fires. The mountain winds are cold. The sheltered valleys hold the sun, then hold the night cold like a bowl of ice. Enormous and red the harvest moon. A white light from a red moon whitens the red leaves. The autumn nights are wild and strange. But the autumn winds that howl down the mountains change and soften inland. Strong soft winds move through the valley ash and oaks. The small dark cedars bend and huddle. The thistles burst gray silky heads, burst and drift. The fields are full of insect sounds, small things pleading and bleating, an endless surfy hum. And then comes the sound of the autumn wind at night, separating leaf from branch, and shuts out the insect singing in the grass. The deer move out into the open fields.

As we move farther and farther from the sun, the fish sink down, the frogs sink down . . . then rise on a warmer day . . . sink back again. The world's still green, still full of drift and flying. Long silver spider strands are launched out, monarch butterflies, veined black and orange, leaves of the locust and wild cherry torn suddenly in the wind; robins migrate, and the long lonely sound of wild geese comes down the sky.

Where do the geese and buzzards go? Where do they *come*? All these departures are arrivals in the seasons of the world. The hummingbird will make it back to Mexico, God willing and nothing of man's come between, and flowers left to feed it there. Wood ducks still haunt the brown polluted streams. The green peninsula of summer still persists. Ailanthus lingering on in a green innocence. Grape leaves large and soft and green.

And then a sudden rib-cracking cold. A freeze too soon. In the morning green leaves fallen all over the ground. A miserable collapse, flabby, flappy green and blackened leaves. The late poke turned to rags. The pond a strange patterned carpet of small green locust leaves, large green grape leaves, yellowing willow leaves. All tree vines—those that had in mind to live forever were blasted white.

As the sun rose, the valley and the trees clear to the horizon were covered with a thick milky blue—a cobra venom spilled for miles. The grass scratched white and silver with the frost. Then began the untimely fall—whole twigs with leaves drifting down from the ailanthus, and the bare twigs, the delicate leafless bones, spiraling down, broken off by the shock of cold. Then the robins came, flocked and flailed, leaves fell, the air was full of twitching and twirling leaves, the ground a curious gray-green mass, a spew—not the autumn harvest of old days. The cold had come too soon, or the leaves had been green too long, swollen, preserved in the too-wet, too-long summer. Intimation, forerunner of another glacial age. The mulberries, which in other years turned a waxy autumn gold, were miserable bleached bits of paper; the hackberries' usual crumbling claw-leaf death was not hastened; but the pawpaws looked as though a fire had flickered through the grove.

In the damp warm days that followed the blast, the curious smell of green death, the silage smell, was everywhere. Gray moths survived, flew up, gray gnats hovered over the gray-green disaster (the quick death hung like gray moss among the living green). Strange snakes emerged, vaguely poisonous-looking but with innocent heads. Giant puffballs boiled out of the earth. Big bleached brains with soft-as-doeskin walls. Calvatia gigantia—bald giants. Were all the spores of one large Calvatia to survive and mature, the second generation alone would be eight hundred times the size of earth. Think about it!

The rainy season in California comes. Grass in the buffalo pens. Weary old pen buffalo eating banana skins. The brown hills start to green. The migrant laborer continues on his round of seasons. He knows the seasons without love. He knows the earth all right. Sometimes he knows it as the floor on which he lives. The gulls come inward on the rains. The gulls are always with us.

The midland states have fields of drying harvests. Vast fields of soybeans begin to brown and dry. Those beans so bushy and belligerent in the warm summer, that great universal basic

Bean—green meat, green protein, life-giving bean—springs up in the spring with that bean vitality, that visible eagerness to grow (far more apparent than in the shoots of corn or wheat). Symbol and fact of the life principle. Simple and two-leafed Bean. Now in the autumn it is brown, nutty, and hairy. Very rough pods—like little animals protecting the hard little beans. And the quail come creeping.

The trees are somber, beautiful, a broodish gathering, around the fields of white aster, the late white butterflies and bees that haunt and hunt the last sweet fields of honey, where the bergamot and teasels dry, and the wild lettuce towers up tall and thin, bearing its soft white ball of seeds, its gnat-ball head.

The autumn world's a place of preparation and of endings. Spinning and hardening goes on, furs thicken and eyes dull. Carapace and cocoon; protection, protection! The hollow stem of wild lettuce and the pith of pokeweed are the high-rise cradles of the solitary wasp. Egg and host, egg and host, laboriously layered one above the other. Nuts are everywhere. Pools of shells. The red-gold squirrels run the trees, gather the iron-black crumbling walnuts. The ground is full of holes. Nut holes, holes open, holes hastily shut. The rich black soil of woodlands without undergrowth is a mass of holes, nuts being buried and dug up, entrances and exits repaired and revised.

The burdock's lusty life is over. It is a brown scaffolding wrapped in black leaves. It crawls with brown-needled burrs. Small ferocious porcupines waiting for a traveler's legs, waiting for entanglement in cats' fur or a pair of socks.

On damp days the Virginia creeper, which has climbed the walnut grove, drips red leaves, blue berries, up and down the long black stems kept thin and frail by crowding, and by the vine's embrace. The poison ivy is orange and red and yellow, extreme colors wildly painted. (Once I saw a face, a human face, fierce and wolf-fanged, with hair wild red-orange of poison ivy leaves in fall.) Later the ivy turns a bronze brown and the berries are white wax—small pearls. The vine flourishes from coast to coast, from north to south, persistent, insistent, part of that vast development, that river of life, parasites, snail flukes, rats and starlings—not in man's pleasure, but following his spoor.

In the mountains of New England trees heat up. Maples hotter and hotter, like iron rising to its final glow of fiery red. The earth a spawned speck of the sun. The anxiety of August is over. The dying is firmed up. Made beautiful and certain. A north wind rags the beech leaves. A cold night wind, and in the morning the grass looks strange, still green and upright, but full of rose and yellow quills, leaves of every size and color, and on the old gray-silver of the fence perch four robins, as though made of red clay overnight.

The crows fly laboring, the hawks soar over the valleys. The giant oaks are rust, the maples an unbelievable burning gold and yellow. When the sunlight falls upon them, pours through them, it is as though one stood in the heart of a cool bonfire, burned and burned and felt only joy—or stood under a vast gold tent of leaves, an expectation of marvelous things to come, good things from some great unknown power. The heart jumps up, expects, believes in promises again, and feels the future good because the Now is gold and good.

Little dark wrens appear mysteriously with continuous cheeping in the reeds and weeds, tiny wrens like bees with bright brown eyes. The yellow-crowned kinglet works the willow leaves, its last bite of bugs in the last leaves, on its way south. A bird so small it hardly seems a bird, so small there is hardly room for the small gold stripe that is called a crown. The kinglets fly, flitter, incessantly as insects, in their insect hunt. They are little olive-green sparks, taking in, giving out—energy made and dispelled without contemplation, to be gone tomorrow, and to be seen arriving somewhere else, as the sign of seasonal change. As the rains in Florida bring a time of planting and a second spring.

There is a squash that looks like flowers. As though those trumpets of the vine had swelled and hardened, bleached white, and then had become fat solid flowers, carved flowers such as one sees on stone pillars or the pews of churches. White flowers for autumn and the coming winter days.

Before the winter season come strange and foggy days. Forerunners of the cold and waiting king. Now in the morning fog and rain, shapes like wild wet goats come down the hills. Down through the fog they come, wave after wave of wild wet goats. Their yellow eyes are cold, their rank wet wool twists in the rain. The mist and fog are bringing them down. Cold, bleating, horned as demons. Ringing the field, pawing the leather leaves, rank and restless. Their pale cold eyes ring the clearing like lamps.

They shake the icy rain from their horns, rain drips from their long white wool. Ice gathers around their hooves. Horned and hungry, fearing the sunrise, they must eat before the sun rises—they must eat or die.

When the sun rises, breaks through the icy fog, there are only prints left, sharp depressions in the damp earth. Winds carry away the scent.

It is still and chill and yellow. The far hills violet, not blue. The snakeroot blossoms have gone gray woolly. Ghost-delicate sheep. Elm leaves yellow and rough. Rough as cattle tongues. Lift up the turtle climbing the steep clay bank. Place him at the top. The turtle speaks: I may not have wished to arrive here. I may have aimed for one of those rock ledges you whizzed me past. Put me back where I was. You are not my Sherpa or my God.

In the north are strange thin clouds. Stretched out like an old one's hair combed over the bluish scalp. Then the hair grows, flies out. Long white hair clouds flying east and west, too thin for snow or rain. Men dredge the pond for bluegills with huge nets. Hunting fish to study the algae on their scales. The dredge, like a huge necklace of brown beads, comes landward with a cargo of bull-poles, starved bluegills, and monster frogs. In hand, they feel cold, cold as ice, but are still gold and green with rusty spots. Put down, they slither sluggishly back into the water. The dredging left a pile of algae, dwarfish fish, and great, slimy, pulsating tad-poles to die on the bank. Food for raccoons, or fertilizer in the spring. The pile of dying fish and tadpoles seemed to wink silver eyes.

In late autumn the mice begin to come inside. The harvest spiders gather. There are no more glowworm lights, and the ferns are heavy with child, as we say—ends borne down, curled up, with brown seeds. Ducks fill the marshes and estuaries. The puzzled robins flock. One day is warm, another cold. To come or stay or go is driving them in circles. They tear up the brown leaves, and a sweet smell rises. The red oaks are still bright and leathery. A few sullen brown-gold hickories keep their leaves, black copper toadstools sprout among the dark green sword ferns fresh and spiky in the damp ravines. In the yellow twilight a hawk flies down among the thorns. (Those thorns that pierce like burning needles and leave blue bruise marks on the human skin.) The maples turn paler in the rain, a pale clean yellow. The rain washes the bark black. A small squirrel hangs upside down, like a bat, from a maple branch. Bends the outermost twigs to eat the maple seeds. What do they taste like? Little rocks in wing cases.

> Now is the season of the dwindling sums,
> The hundreds shrunken down to ones.
> One frog,
> One purple leaf, one frosted pear,
> Last wedge of calling geese,
> Then bleached and empty air.

Darkness comes early in the valleys and the deep ravines.

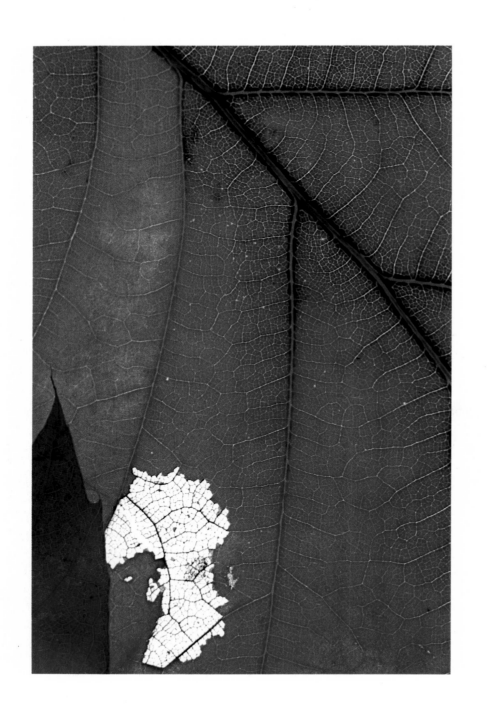

WINTER

In the Midwest the winter does not *begin*. It does not roar in like a mad motorcyclist, chains waving, jackknife bared. It comes and goes like an icy tide around the long peninsula of autumn. Bewildered birds fly southward, then return, go back again. There are no graceful endings. The rip and howl of wind is all. Evictions. Buryings. The bone twigs scattered, leaves driven into ground. The hurled-down web and lichen nests of little birds return to moss. Rain sluices down the tunnels under earth; the late-born field mice drown.

There seems no rock bottom anywhere, no place from which there is no place to go but up. (There are oceans beneath the ocean floor.) The rain, falling through the yellow leaves on the ground, makes them shine and flash, so sun-bright even in the early winter gloom that one expects to see a rainbow in the darkening sky. There are always late flowers somewhere in the early winter hours. Violets under their own great heart-shaped sheltering leaves. Late gold dandelions in some sunny little cove where mice admire. And strange flowering of pears, white blossoms blooming on bare tree branches, heavy with a hundred small bronze pears.

Then through the sweet wet leaves the cold comes moving. The savage snout of cold. That quivering frosted thing like a pig's nose.

The winter marshlands carry thin crusts of frozen mud that sink underfoot; the plumes of marsh grass rise around as tall as trees. Ducks fly up, a sound of wet sheets tearing from their flight. From pods and housings seeds leave home in their cold and curious ways. Drift. Drop. Some bang down, hitting branches, bouncing off trunks, roll in the leaves, are gathered up in squirrel teeth or weasel snouts. Some drift awhile, wander out to sea, die in its vast gray heaving, or glue themselves to knife fin of a shark. The bursting of gray milkweed pods, the soft silver explosions send delicate parachutes flying over neglected lands. Lands where the long grass has fallen down in gray humps. A river of silver-gray grass, and in this river thousands of porcupines, old gray grass porcupines, seem swimming. Swimming on night and day. Never arriving. Grass porcupines with wet gray quills.

In the early dark, in the warm brown evenings of early winter, moths are still flying up from the wet brown leaves. The fragrance of leaves scuffed in the twilight is more haunting than the fragrance of bread or flowers. Withered apples in the orchard cling for the animals' last harvest, and on the wild roses there is orange fruit. Rich scrunchy fruit for the bears and quail and pheasants. And mountain sheep eat the fruit of roses.

The swallows leave the north, go back to Texas and Mexico, but the great jays stay on—blue against the brown leaves, blue against the first snow, loud in the vegetable silence, mocking the hawks. One jay can fill a desert valley, make its presence known as far as eye can see or ear hear. Flying from scrub oak to scrub oak with its passionate complaints.

Late fungus, fawn-colored or gray as smooth cattle hides, sprouts in the woods, and the leathery lichen is ringed with moss. There are few things colder-looking than these naked fleshy fungi trembling in the first winter winds and mud.

The shapes of trees emerge. Take fantastic forms. Wild broken-antlered deer. Heads of moose and goat. Beasts, decaying crocodiles, saurian things. Take the shape of naked human forms, grasping and clinging. Roots penetrating. The cold enormous passion of tree locked in tree. Stones gathered up like children, wrapped forever in the arms of roots.

In the mountains the vast ceremony of the snow begins. The northern winters have an almost intolerable majesty. A terrifying giant beauty that makes all else seem small and pale. The weight and power of snow, the glass-white glitter and glare of snow, cover rocks, earth, and water.

Under the long winter war between sun and snow, the animals survive. Burrow, grow slow and shaggy, herd together, seek sheltered valleys. Or, like the bears, grow shaggy, grow slow, sink down in caves. A lot of sleeping goes on, under the snow, inside gray trees, or deep in the earth. A lot of slow cavernous breathing. But even more of life—running and killing and eating, in small damp tunnels. Mice and weasels and fierce little bad-luck shrews.

The cold makes flowers and ferns of ice. The long blue shadows of the trees stretch out across the snow. In the wind the shadows move across the snow, leap back and forth like tethered hounds. The cold and limited life of the shadows.

And there is the beauty of silence. Snowfields stretching fold over, fold to a white horizon. The arctic owl drifts down through forests of snow in silence. Valleys are covered with hoar frost, frozen mist, and no wind moves in a silent dawn. In the stillness, as the sun rises over the white snow, silent as the snow, a red fox runs. A red fox shining with gold hairs in the winter sun.

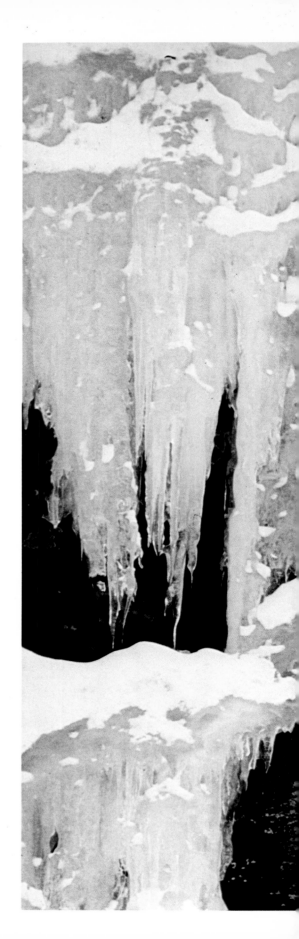

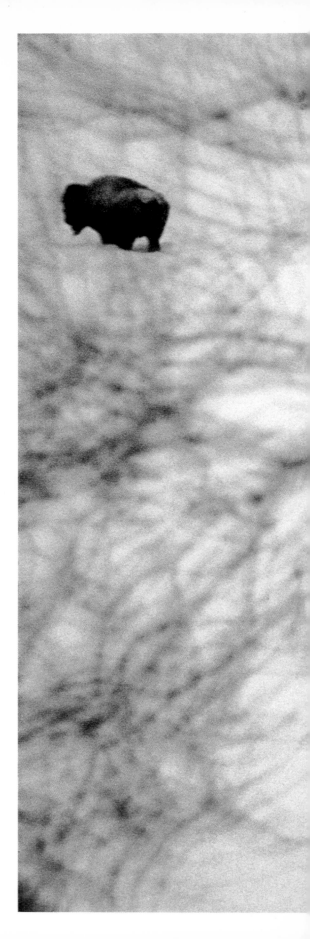

Winter is a strange, stark bone time. Its blessings and its burdens are too hard. Its magnificent silences and wildness we destroy wherever we can find them. "The wolves of Cuan-wood get neither rest nor sleep in their lairs . . ." the Irish poet wrote of a cold winter in the tenth century. "The little wren cannot find shelter in her nest on the slope of Lon." . . . The wolves find neither rest nor sleep nor life in most of the world today . . . but the wren survives. Chirps cheerily on.

By midwinter the sun is cold and white as a diamond. Earth has moved to the farmost limit of its flight. It is as cold as it will ever be, and one knows that it is winter. Winter—that time when one begins to feel the bones around the eyes.

The pheasant step softly, with delicate precision, across the crusted snow. The quail move with nervous caution, but the cardinals flock recklessly, light, flare up as small red flames.

The dark comes early, but great brilliant crimson sunsets come. Great earth-retreats. Earth whirls away from flaming crimson skies, from the melted gold, volcanic heat, from gigantic shows that cool down fast. The last light is a cold gray-yellow. A pewter sky.

All endings are beginnings. All beginnings end. There is no end. The winter ice melts into water. Long water fingers that reach out and touch the coming spring. The March winds howl, the mountain snow begins to crack. In sheltered places of the continents, the ancient plant, the equisetum, the oldest plant, pushes up through clay and sand again.

Cold and blue are the mountains. Old trees, the old men of the mountains, stand in loneliness along the ridges of the world.

PHOTOGRAPHY

It is a blessed thing to be a photographer. To be able to continue an attitude of childlike discovery into adult existence can be perceived only as a gift toward the individual's spiritual survival.

The driving force of the photographer is the need to discover. The choice of an arena to seek out new imagery often calls for forethought. A specific theme with considerable graphic potential seems to be the rule of thumb for most accomplished photographers. In recent years I have pursued two themes. One is the sun in nature, and the other the four seasons.

My gravitation toward nature as my primary preoccupation in photography seems to have an organic flow. The subject is rich with images and magical visions, a photographer's dream. Often as I stand in the forest, I am held by a feeling of reverence, a peace that contributes greatly to the penetration of the unknown.

A compulsive need for changing images forced me from the deadening familiarities of urban asphalt and concrete composites to discover the ephemeral expressions of brush-stroked landscapes and the power of nature's details subtly revealed in infinite ways. Equipped with 35mm single-lens reflex cameras and a collection of lenses from 21mm to 500mm, I trip, stumble, trek, and climb into a playground of promise. The cameras are easy and light to handle, particularly for moments when the body and eye adjust to the fleeting changes in the environment. Winds bend reeds into postures of classical Chinese-scroll detail. Clouds briefly part, emitting rays that focus on distant carved forms hidden normally by atmospheric haze. Shapes, colors, and textures are transferred to film to the accompaniment of my intent anticipation.

The changing seasons enhance discovery. For the familiar surprises me with lovely disguises. Ice and snow sculpt new façades on the old, now hidden secrets of sleeping landscapes. Counteracting a winter death, a fern's muscular change inspires the eye to retain a virile expression of spring. I have clicked with wonderment at the struggle of a beetle in a tightrope-walking display. I have tried to learn about life from the rich autumn expression of leaves so close to death. The luminescent beauty of a dragonfly makes me pray. Sun-etched red sand dunes with their textured patterns remind me of my infancy in the scheme of things. A warm feeling of thanks often rises with the acceptance I luckily get from a wild animal who poses for a portrait to be taken by his brother. The searching culminates in gratitude and retention. A preserved image is another way of saying, "Life is good."

I must confess that part of the joy experienced while out in nature is attributable to the lens I view through and the disciplines of the camera's frame. Optical translation and the dynamics of composing enhance the moment. The rest is totally subjective.

There are few manufacturer's rules that govern or interfere with my pleasures in the field. Applying the classic principles of composition and light, I try to make a statement that is articulate and invested with sufficient drama and graphic vitality to survive in a two-dimensional form. No mechanical manipulation dictates my approach. For me, beauty seems to be less difficult to find when technology is reduced to the barest of existences. The right moment of contact is a state of brief and intense meditation. The creative communion cannot be disrupted by more than a short click of the shutter. My energies concentrated through the penetrating lens often create a sense of mergence with subject, and thereby a realization of the oneness of life. Eye pressed tight against the window and led by the lens's shifting focus, the journey goes deep into wondrous stages of pure revelation. There are no words heard. Lines, colors, and movements touch something inside me, and I am happily lost, without an f stop in my head.

The sun is always shadow-shaping some place, some creature, and some thing. Enough to motivate a life's tour and assure any photographer that light in all its variances will assist the pursuit for growth.

We have all shared in an encounter with beauty. According to the Taos Indians, this is the ultimate intention of man.

> Out of the dark into Light
> The people were created for Beauty
> The head, the mind, to think Beauty
> The eyes to see Beauty
> The ears to hear Beauty
> The tongue to speak Beauty
> The hands to work in Beauty
> The heart to bear love towards all.

—Creation Chant of Taos Indians

Dennis Stock/1974